ONE CANDLE

BY EVE BUNTING
ILLUSTRATED BY K. WENDY POPP

JOANNA COTLER BOOKS
An Imprint of HarperCollins*Publishers*

If the soul of this book is rendered well at all in your opinion, it is due entirely to the endearing faces of my friends and family. They have helped me to envision Ms. Bunting's characters with resonance and authenticity. I am deeply grateful to our charming grandmother Eliane Kiami; for the patience and grace of Rose, Zoe, Lisa, and Jesse Birnbaum; for the charismatic Cliff, Laura, Jane, and the irrepressible Drew Broffman; for the generosity of "Aunt" Dorothy and "Grandfather" Frank Leicht, Dennis Noskin, and the Skriloffs. To Madeline, Jessica, my Zoe and Amanda, I thank you for your willingness to imagine dark places with empathy. For the kitchen of Bradley's of Larchmont, the abundant Hanukkah dinner catered by Stanz, and the advice of Larchmont Temple, many thanks again.

—K.W.P.

One Candle   Text copyright © 2002 by Edward D. Bunting and Anne E. Bunting, Trustees of the Edward D. Bunting and the Anne E. Bunting Family Trust   Illustrations copyright © 2002 by K. Wendy Popp   Printed in the U.S.A.   All rights reserved. www.harperchildrens.com   Library of Congress Cataloging-in-Publication Data   Bunting, Eve.   One candle / by Eve Bunting ; illustrated by K. Wendy Popp.   p.   cm.   Summary: Every year a family celebrates Hanukkah by retelling the story of how Grandma and her sister managed to mark the day while in a German concentration camp.   ISBN 0-06-028115-4 — ISBN 0-06-028116-2 (lib. bdg.)   [1. Hanukkah — Fiction.   2. Concentration camps—Fiction.]   I. Popp, Wendy, ill. II. Title. PZ7.B91527 On   2002   [E]—dc21   2001047205   Typography by Alicia Mikles   1 2 3 4 5 6 7 8 9 10 ❖ First Edition

To Donna Curtis and Martha van der Veen, with love

—E.B.

For Wynn, Zoe, and Bill, my own candles

—K.W.P.

THIS HANUKKAH IS LIKE EVERY OTHER ONE.

Our house is filled with food and family and delicious cooking smells. Our great-aunt Rose is here. She's Grandma's sister. There's Mom and Dad, we three kids, and my uncle and his family.

When Grandma and Grandpa arrive at our house, Dad gets to hug them first. Grandma brings the potato.

When I was little, I thought it was to eat. Or to grate for the latkes that Mom makes. But it isn't.

Grandma puts the big, brown potato on the plate in the middle of the table, and Great-Aunt Rose leans across to touch it with a trembling finger. Her glasses are misted over.

"Poor Great-Aunt Rose!" my cousin Nancy whispers. "She's crying again this year."

"You'd cry too, if you were her," my big sister Ruth says.

After sunset we light one candle in the menorah with the shammash for the first night of
Hanukkah, say special prayers, and take our places at the table.

Dad piles our plates with sliced brisket and gravy. Mom passes the latkes and the sour
cream and the dishes mounded high with applesauce.

The candles in the menorah burn low, and shadows tremble on the ceiling. The table buzzes with conversation. I love all our holidays when we're together like this. But maybe I love Hanukkah most of all.

After we've eaten, Mom looks at Grandma. "I think it's time, Mama."

Grandma nods.

Then Dad goes in the kitchen and brings back the things Grandma will need. Grandma takes the small knife and begins to hollow the potato.

We are all very quiet, even my cousin Baby Sam, who has been fussing all through dinner trying to pull off his bib.

We watch as Grandma piles the small pieces of scooped-out potato onto her plate.

"Tell us now about the bad time, Mama," Mom says. Her voice is so soft and loving.

We lean forward. We know this story by heart, but we want to hear it again. To us, this story *is* Hanukkah.

Grandma takes Great-Aunt Rose's hand. "Well, it happened when we were young. We were separated from our families and put into a camp. It was called Buchenwald. That was in Germany. There was a war on at the time, and the Germans didn't like the Jews."

"Why?" my little sister, Bitsy, asks, and I remember how, one by one, we'd all asked that question. Baby Sam will probably ask it next.

Grandma shrugs, and Grandpa says, "The Germans didn't like a lot of people. It wasn't only the Jews."

Grandpa wasn't in a camp. He met Grandma afterward, when she came to America.

"The camp was like the worst prison you could imagine," Grandma says. "We were always hungry, always cold. There were seven women in our barracks. But at least Rose and I were together."

Great-Aunt Rose begins to whisper the names of the other women, the way you'd say a prayer.

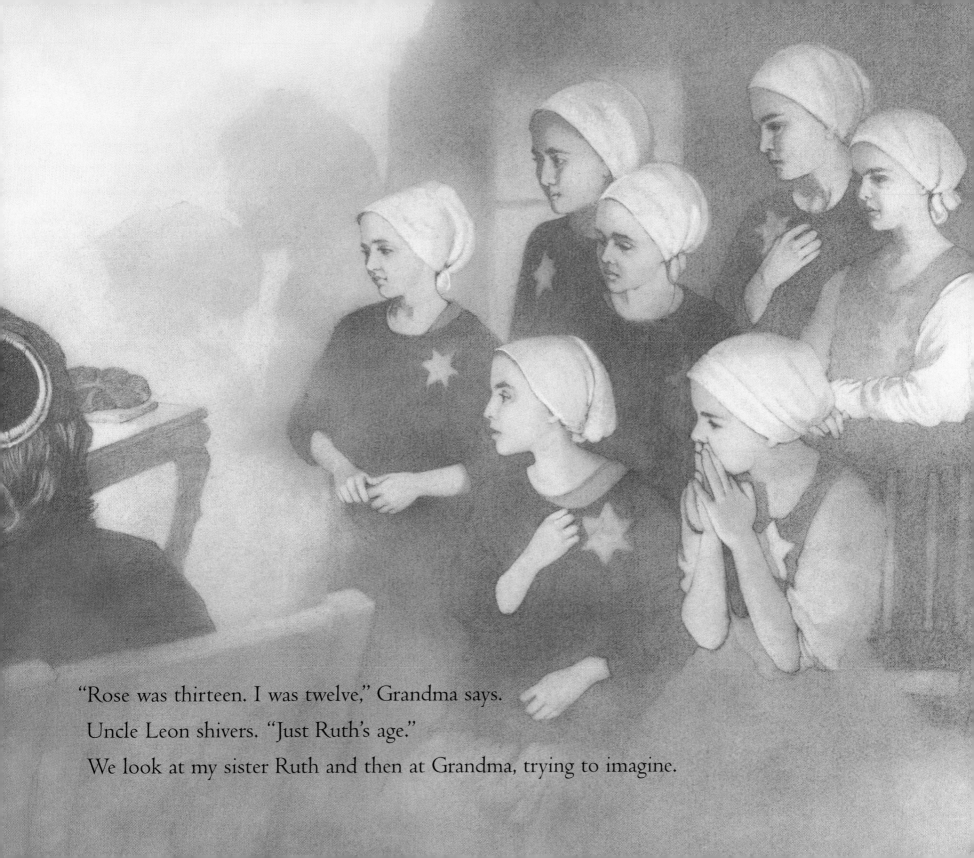

"Rose was thirteen. I was twelve," Grandma says.

Uncle Leon shivers. "Just Ruth's age."

We look at my sister Ruth and then at Grandma, trying to imagine.

"The older women worked in the fields," Grandma continues. "Rose and I worked in the kitchens. We were small and thin. It's a marvel they even kept us. We helped cook for the officers." Grandma leans back in her chair and closes her eyes. Her chin quivers. "All that wonderful food. None of it for us."

I look around the table. I am full from Mom's delicious cooking. And there are still leftovers. I can't imagine going hungry.

"Hanukkah was coming," Grandma says. "We knew because we kept the dates on a hidden piece of paper. Working there in the kitchen I had an idea. Little by little I smuggled things out. A blob of margarine in a scrap of paper, small enough to hide in my hand. Two matches. And on the day before Hanukkah, a potato. Not as big a one as this. I brought it out under my skirt." Grandma puts her hand over her heart. "Oh, I was so frightened. I thought my chest would burst with fear. The guard at the door looked at me so suspiciously. Aunt Rose walked beside me. She gave me courage."

Great-Aunt Rose shakes her head. "I had no courage to give you, Lilly."

"You held me up," Grandma says.

"What would they have done if they'd caught you?" Ruth asks.

Great-Aunt Rose gives a little moan.

"There, there. We were all right," Grandma says. She squeezes her sister's hand.

"When we got back to the barracks, the women couldn't believe what I'd done. A potato! Heaven! Were we going to eat it right away? No. That wasn't why I took the risk."

Grandma looks around the table at each of us. We know why she took the risk.

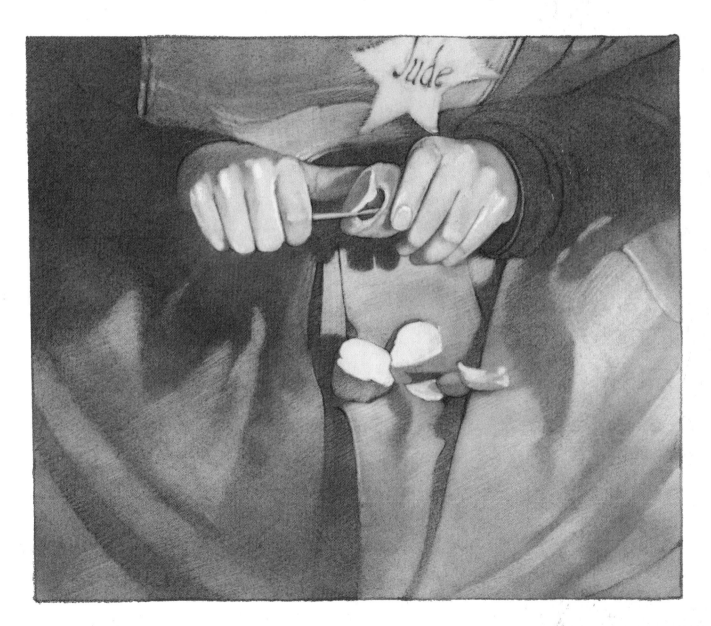

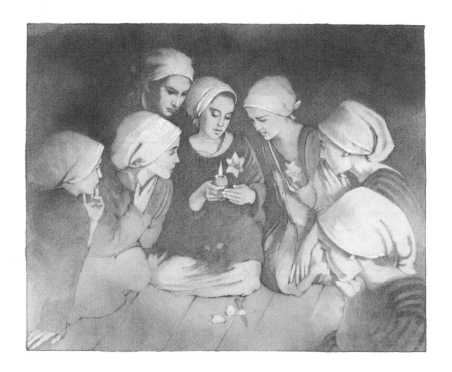

"I hollowed out part of that potato, the way I did with this one." Grandma touches the potato and stares down at it. "We ate the pieces I'd saved—"

Nancy interrupts, "Raw? Yuk!"

Grandma smiles and nods her head. "Delicious! Better than any candy. Then we put the margarine I'd stolen into the potato, pulled a thread from Rose's skirt to make a wick, and lit the flame." She pauses. "We had one candle for Hanukkah.

"That Hanukkah candle lifted us," Grandma says, and there are tears in her eyes. "It lifted us to the stars."

Bitsy screws up her face. "How could it lift you, Grandma?"

"In our minds, sweetheart. In our hearts."

Now we watch as Grandma pours oil into the potato and lights the wick I've made from twisted threads. We have a flame. We have a candle.

Grandma wipes away her tears and we all stand up.

"May I take it?" I ask.

"Yes," Grandma says.

I set the candle on the windowsill, and it glows back on itself in the dark glass.

We go outside. Dad has switched off the house lights, and the Hanukkah candle has burned itself away. On the windowsill is this one, steady flame.

My sister Ruth whispers close to my ear, "Why do you think Grandma wants to do this every year?"

I shrug my shoulders because I don't know for sure. But I think it has to do with being strong in the bad time and remembering it in the good time. And for the women in Grandma's barracks and the others who didn't live to come out.

Grandpa passes the little glasses of sweet wine to the grown-ups and the grape juice to us. We raise the glasses toward the flame.

"L'chayim," Grandma says. "To life!"

"To life!" we chant.

And in that moment we are lifted to the stars.